WHO AM I REALLY ?

THE ULTIMATE TRUTH

BY

SIVA

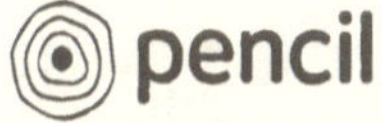 pencil

ISBN 978-93-5438-956-6

Published in India 2020 by Pencil

A brand of

One Point Six Technologies Pvt. Ltd.

123, Building J2, Shram Seva Premises,

Wadala Truck Terminal, Wadala (E)

Mumbai 400037, Maharashtra, INDIA

E connect@thepencilapp.com

W www.thepencilapp.com

DISCLAIMER: *The opinions expressed in this book are those of the authors and do not purport to reflect the views of the Publisher.*

Author biography

I am Truth seeker and the researcher of Consciousness.

Contents

LET SELF ENQUIRY BEGIN...06

LET SELF ENQUIRY BEGIN

Contents

1. Who Am I Really ?

2. Truth Behind Time, Reality and Evolution !

3. The Ultimate Truth

4. Life Depends On Nature

5. Find The Source (Realize Who You Are!)

6. Awaken Mind

WHO

AM

I

REALLY ?

LET SELF ENQUIRY BEGIN

I Just close my eyes and imagine!, Now I am surrounding with my friends and relatives and people all around.

He says, She says, They says, He like, and dislike, They like and dislike.

They said what I should do.

They said what am I doing.

That's good for me, That's bad for my health,
mind, soul and so on.

That makes me worth living.
This makes me right or wrong/ good or bad.
Everyone judges me, values me, evaluate me.
Everyone just simply put their destiny on me.
But no one knows himself or herself truly.

And I Say
I'm going to do this thing or that thing.
I just need to keep on wait for authority of others.
None of my knowledge has been made by my own.
Everything is said to me by others, friends,
relatives, parents, teachers.

(Nothing is a getting of my own knowledge.)
All knowledge came from others.
I am just a second hand person.
I am just a photocopy of others.
Now i am going to work like a labour.
Because they taught, they are also working like
labour that's why they taught, they trained
me like being in a circus.
They said life is a race.
They said life is a competition!
So go run, run, run.
They compare me with others.

(Comparison, Competition Kills you,
it breeds suicide.)

They asked me what you become.
They tell me this is your family.
They tell me what to desire.
They tell me what to do.
They tell me what to think.
They tell me what to feel.
They tell me to salute.
They tell me to obey.
They tell me which country is.
They tell me what country is.
They tell me which religion is.
They tell me what religion is.
They tell me which tradition is.
They tell me what tradition is.
They tell me what to pray.
They tell me how to play.
They tell tell me where I see.
They tell me what to eat.
They tell me what to wear.
They tell me when to sleep.
They tell me when to awake.
They tell me what to study.

They tell me what to read.

They tell me when to play.

They tell me what to play.

They order me, and so on...

They say so, because they just followed millions of era, so They don't know who they really are!!.

Conditions, Conditions, Conditions!!

All are conditioning me, on my every nature.

There is no noble or better conditioning; all conditioning are painful.

Separateness, dividing ourselves from some belief, tradition, religion.

It breeds violence.

They just treat me like cattle.

Like sheep, cow, and so on.

(Now should I Praise or Blame Others!??)

QUESTION : Now I Ask Myself WHO AM I ?

ANSWER : Who Others Think I AM !

DON'T LIVE SOMEONE'S DESTINY - THAT'S NOT LIVING !!.

{It is very easy to confirm to what your society or your parents and your teachers tell you. That is a safe and easy way of existing but This is not living...

To live is to find out for yourself what is True!.}

(Sentimentality and emotionalism are the most destructive things.)

I can't feel The earth, air, or universe. I am just filled with what others opinion. I depend on others. That is not really what I am!!..

Lets Begin to Enquiry

And now I just close my eyes and imagine now I am surrounding with no one except all material things. I am just alone only.

Now I can feel the earth, air, but not universe.

Now I think what am I.

What I want.

What I have.

I have to fill me with my own ambition. My own desire arises.

I'm going to do this or that thing.

That's going to be fulfilled in my life.

Maybe I am a Scientist.

Maybe I am an Inventor.

Maybe I am an engineer.

Maybe I am a doctor or artist, and so on...

Then I Say

This is my life.

This is my house.

This is my family.

This is my property.

This is my nation.

This is my country.

This is my phone.

This is my car.

This is my dress.

This is mine, That is mine, and so on...

All I have possess things.

I want to become this or that.

I want to go to live in this or that country.

I want to serve my country or people.

I am independent person.

I have some identity to myself this or that.

Personification.

Now I go to where ever I want.

To do what ever I like.

Now I Think

What to feel.

What to do.

What to eat.

What to wear.

When to sleep.

When to wake.

Where to go.

When to come.

Now I think Everything is done by me.

But

It is not me.

It is my pure ego.

My ego drives me.

My envy drives me crazy.

Now I think I am the master of my own destiny.

(Now I Praise or Blame Only Myself.)

But is this worth living?

I really know who I am?

Do I really live freely?

<u>QUESTION</u> : Now I Ask Myself WHO AM I ?

<u>ANSWER</u> : Who I Think I AM.

(I think I am this or that)

{Ambition is the outcome of an unhappy person
not of a happy person. To do what you like, is that
freedom ? No it is not !.

There is great happiness in not wanting, in not being something, in not going somewhere.}

Lets Begin to Enquiry

And now I just close my eyes and imagine, now I am in some deep forest, There is no people's surrounding me, I am alone with only trees, river, flowers, butterflies, waterfalls, hills, birds, rainbows. Surrounding with all and only nature.

Now it is totally different dimension.

I can feel the gravity.

I can feel the earth, air, water, five elements.

Not universe.

But I feel something rare, extraordinary feelings arising within me.

I see waterfalls, butterfly, trees, cuckoo singing and so on.. of all nature.

Now I feel complete Silence.

Now I feel Peace.

Now I enjoy myself totally.

Now I express myself completely.

Bliss is overflowing through myself.

Now I feel aloneness is joyful.

Now slowly, slowly my ego is dissolved.

My ambition is dissolved.

Nothing to do.

And Now

(There is no division, no more religion, no tradition..

Not at all.

Because I can feel everything is connected.)

Now

Duality disappeared.

Unity remains.

There is no more ego.

Ego dissolved into this vast silence.

There is neither comparison nor competition.

All are dissolved into nothingness.

Now

I can hear, see, smell, taste everything very clearly

I know my very nature is Bliss!.

Happiness is surrounding me without any external
activities.

I am happy with no reason.

I am simply happy like a child.

Everything is fresh and new.

I observe my own breath very clearly.

Breathing in and out.

How it works ?

How it functions ?

Who works ?

Just Watching my own breath.

QUESTION : Now I Ask Myself WHO AM I ?

ANSWER : I don't know WHO I AM ?

{It is far more important to understand yourself, the constant changing of facts about yourself, than to meditate, in order to find god, have visions, sensations and other forms of entertainment.}

Then The Original Enquiry Begin

And Now I Just close my eyes and not imagine because imagination has cease and Now this time I am not going anywhere outside, Now I am going very very deep inside me. (Like going through space, going to empty space deeper and deeper no one is there, no object is there, only emptiness.)

Suddenly I felt like sleeping.

But it's not asleep.

It's awakening.

The me is absent.

There is no observer.

Thought is gone.

Thinking is cease.

Mind is gone.

Time is gone.

Now

I am entirely alone.

Utterly great silence.

No mind.

Just emptiness.

Stillness.

No thought, no imagination utterly nothing.

Then I am afraid of nothing.

Afraid of silence.

And slowly slowly fear will vanish in this vast space
of silence.

Emptiness is with in and out.

Tranquility.

Now

I observe everything.

The the observer is observed.

I listen clearly.

Watchful.

Alert.

I don't know where I am.

Just totally different dimension.

I am gone.

Just mingling with the space.

Like a rain drop mingling, where it rise in the ocean.

I, is dissolved in this vast space of silence.

just emptiness, utter silence.

Seamless, unnameable, immeasurable.

Suddenly I realize

WHO I AM

Then the very question Who Am I is dissolves.

Dissolve in to nothingness.

No one is answering.

All question is ceased.

Thinking is stopped.

Thoughts are ceased.

Feelings are ceased.

Language too ceased.

All are gone.

Mind is utterly empty.

Body senses starts dissolving.

No - Mind

No - Body

Serenity

Then only the Truth is encounter.

Truth reveals itself.

The word the self which means the core of all.

Enters into the Heart.

Heart of universe.

Core of the universe.

Core of life.

Let silence take you to the core of life.

I, doesn't exist.

I, is neither everything nor nothing.

No self is the real self.

All are just imagination or memory.

It's just reflection of the mind.

All are just fading away.

Nothing remains.

only quietness and stillness.

The self is the source of all things, only size and
shapes are different.

If this realized, all forms are suddenly disappeared.

Enter into the formless.

one is all.

All is none.

One is love.

Love is god.

God is all.

All is one.

I get dissolved and merged with one.

There are no other's, whatever you see outside

is your own reflection.

Your mind is creating all those.

Oneness is the secret of everything.

Helping yourself, you help everybody else.

The universe is within.

Just harmony with the universe.

There is no destiny.

There is no master.

Nothing to be done.

Nowhere to go.

Simply - live - breath.

(Now I Praise or Blame No One.)

Because I is dead.

I am neither body nor mind.

I am neither thought nor feeling.

The word I am is oneness.

The source.

The being.

The existence.

Pure consciousness.

Aloneness.

Awareness.

Stillness.

Timeless.

Witness.

Formless.

Bliss.

Peace.

Self.

Enough identification to this or that.

Identification dissolves into silence.

Dis-identify remains.

No more words can describe.

How can you describe wordless state.

Wordless encounter.

All images are ceased.

Words or images is nothing but the by product of thought.

If the words or chatting or images is there then the mind is there.

So it can't be there.

It is there.

It is always there.

When the mind is still.

And then Truth reveals itself.

It is here and now.

It is only when the mind is silent than the truth
of what is unfolds.

In this silence, everything is related to everything else.

In this stillness, everything is connected.

Real relation happens in silence.

Real communication happens in silence.

-/-
/-/

TRUTH BEHIND TIME, REALITY AND EVOLUTION !!

"Everything we call REAL is made of things that
cannot be regarded as REAL" – BOHR

CHAOS :- Time and Reality are two separate things/
different things but, that is not true.

TRUTH :- Time and Reality are the same thing!

Reality exists only in the present time and therefore,
changes by moment-to-moment.

Time and Reality are the same things working like
fabric (space-time) inseparable.

"Time is Reality"

"Reality is dependent on Time"

Everything/whole thing is just a time lapse.

An art of time lapse.

An art of reality.

Timelines/Realities.

There are different timelines/Realities.

And Timelines are dependent on Space.

Because we all know space-time (4D) are fabric.

" Don't let people rush you with their timelines/
Realities"

"Live your life in your own Timelines/Realities"

Don't compare your time/reality to others.

There is no comparison between the sun and
the moon.

They shine when it's their time.

And now we all clear about "Reality depends
on Time"

Einstein says: "Time is Relative". Time is nothing
but a stubborn Illusion.

So, If Time is an illusion, then what is reality?

Reality is also an illusion!!!

Einstein also said: "Reality merely an illusion, albeit
a very persistent one"

"What is normal for the spider, is chaos for the fly" –
Adams

So, what is Reality? There is no such thing as

'REALITY'

And Hence we are all caught up on an illusion?

Trapped in a time/ an illusion ?

Could we be able to go beyond of all Time-Space-
Reality / merely an illusion ?

Is it possible? Yes.

"Time is an illusion of the mind" – Immanuel kant

"Reality is created by the mind. We can change our
reality by changing our mind" – Plato

Then what is Mind?

Humans are fully moulded with emotions but what
lies beyond those emotions?

We are all shaped up by our Thoughts.

We are all reactions of our feelings.

But see, "Thoughts would come and go

Feelings must come and go

To find out what it is that remains" –
Ramana Maharishi

What it's remains is far more important
than anything.

Einstein said : "Look deep into Nature and then you
will understand everything better"

" Nature is not a by product of God. Nature is God"

"Philosophy is empty if it isn't based on science.

Science discovers, philosophy interprets."

"Philosophy means the love of Truth" – J.K

Both philosophy and science are exploring the same Truth.

{UNDERSTAND + DISCOVER = INVENTION } :- CREATIVE

Creativity is an Art .

Art of Living :- (this is what makes you Alive otherwise you're just living as a slave like any pet animal)

Because animals are already designed but Humans are the only beings designed by itself.

First of all you don't know about yourself completely then, how could it be possible to discover or invent something that is never ever seen before.

How could it be possible?

Is it possible? Yes.

First you must Completely understand who you are and what you are.

Must Discover you to yourself totally and intensely.

And then Invention comes out of their own way.

This is called Creativity .

INNOVATION flows from **INVENTION** .

This whole process is called **EVOLUTION** .

We think Evolution. We are all talking about evolution.

We are So much evolved physically but that's not enough.

Physically we are evolved such as Bullock cart to aeroplane; hut to steel house.

But psychologically?

Is there any psychological evolution taken place? NO.

We are all on the same level of animal conscious level.

Because, If there is any psychological evolution taken place, then

Why are we separated like animals?

Air, water, land, fire these are all common Right? Then

Why we separate our earth?

Why we have army?

Why we fight with each other, killing each other like animals?

Where is compassion? Where is love? Where is peace?

Peace, love, compassion only comes out by words but not actually.

Actually do we all live in peace, love, compassion? NO.

We do not live in peace, love, compassion.

Psychologically/Inwardly we carry hundreds of, thousands of old traditions, cultures, all over dogmas, propaganda from ancient age to modern age until now.

This traditions, cultures, races and nation come and pass away but mans consciousness is remains.

We all live in anxiety, depression, greed, lust, antagonism, egotism, envy, fear, anger, suppress, superstition, pleasure, sorrow, comparison, competition, division, ambition, violence, brutal, distinctive merit, abuse, gossip, lying, killing and so on..

We live in this society and we obviously see how cruel we are.

The world we see is an outward projection of an inward condition.

Everything we experience is an outward projection of our inward state of mind.

This psychologically/Inwardly war is not yet complete.

Is there any possibility could we completely end this psychological war?Is there radical transformation taking place in our behaviour? Could man completely free from all of his dogmas, propaganda?

Not only physically but psychologically?

Is there any psychological mutation taking place?

Is it possible?

Yes.

How it is possible?

When it is possible?

When a man fully understands himself.

Realizes his own mind totally and completely.

When we understand our Sixth Sense totally.

When we realized our Sixth Sense completely.

We all talk about the Sixth sense, but I don't know how many of us know exactly what it is.

'PERCEPTION' Is Our SIXTH Sense. PERCEPTION IS INSIGHT. Humans Only Have 'INSIGHT'.

But many of us do not use it. A Very Few Know it and use it well in our everyday life.

When we are AWARE of it. When we use our Sixth Sense in our daily life.

And that Sixth Sense leads to another / upgrades.

It can be Evolved. That is 'WISDOM'

Out of that Wisdom comes Compassion.

'COMPASSION' is the highest quality of all our senses.

Compassion for all being; not only for our family, our neighbours, our friends or for human being.

There was no salvation without compassion for every other being.

Compassion is the only path to salvation.

Only in the sense of compassion, we differ from animals.

Otherwise there is nothing difference between animals and humans.

<u>**Buddha**</u> said : "Mind is Everything".

<u>**Einstein**</u> said : " Everything is connected"

And I say: "The Mind is connected with Everything

Or

Everything is connected with the Mind".

So,

" The MIND is a key to the Evolution"

<u>**ACTUALLY**</u> :-

PEACE – LOVE – COMPASSION are not
different entities.

When there is Compassion in the Heart.
There is Love.

When there is Love in the Heart. There is Peace.

When there is Peace in the Heart. There is
Intelligence in the Mind.

Then such a mind itself becomes sacred.

Only Such a mind knows what freedom is.

Intelligence is Compassion.

Intelligence is Love.

Intelligence is Peace.

Otherwise there is no Intelligence at all.

-/-
/-/

<u>THE ULTIMATE TRUTH</u>

It is hard to believe that you are everything!

But actually, what takes place?

You don't need to believe something which you never experienced.

But you need to enquire yourself, observe everything around you and your whole attention to the fact of what is.

When you are totally in the present moment, in this compete attention of something which becomes interesting of anything you do or work or listening any music or reading, be it anything.

If you're reading this with your complete attention, thought never comes, thinking is ceased.

Then what takes place?

Only stillness! Silence! Comes to your whole being.

In this utter silence, only happens when you are completely attentive to the present moment.

In this stillness, you are no more, you don't exist Which means identification. Only seeing and listening remains.

Seeing this text and listening you whole around.

Everything you can see, hear clearly when your mind is completely still, when you have compete attention to the present moment.

In this complete stillness, you become one with the whole.

You are neither the body nor the mind.

You are neither boy nor girl.

You are awareness

You are consciousness.

You are pure being.

In this silence you related to everything else.

In this complete silence you are everything, simultaneously you are nothing.

You are formless like a pure sky, vast space.

In this present moment, which is constantly changing.

So you are!

You are just watching, listening, seeing, observing, witnessing.

You are awaken!

Only present moment is real, otherwise are all illusion whether it is imagination or memory.

Nature is silence! Stillness!

When you observe, watching the marvellous sunset or waterfalls or rainbow or huge mountain region or moon light reflects through the vast ocean or night clouds with moon.

As you watching anything of nature.

So very stil you really become part of everything.

You were everything.

When you observe the nature, there is complete stillness.

In this stillness, you are unchanging.

Great peace with eternal bliss comes into your
being from the unknown.

Unnameable, immeasurable comes into your being
or it is always there, if your mind is very quietness
and complete still.

You cannot possible to describe it but you can feel it.

How can silence be explained in words?

Everything is made of atoms.

Everything is made of universe.

Everything is made of the same source.

Thus, the nature has construct the whole thing
(living and non living).

This universe, this earth has structured
Every living things.

Every living being is a molecular structure
of universe by itself.

Human being is a complete molecular structure
of universe made by itself.

Each cell contains every living being.

Every cell in our body is a universe of its own its
intelligent, its complete.

Every atom contains entire universe.

We are all a miniature of universe.

Human body is very rare body because you are the
only being can feel the wholeness, the divinity.

You are complete molecular structure of universe.

You are divine.

That's why you are capable of understand everything!

You are capable of understand the wholeness both inwardly and outwardly.

I call it Spiritual Science.

Spiritual is nothing but a pure Science.

Spiritual – Explore the Truth Inwardly.

Science – Explore the same Truth Outwardly.

Both are True!

We need to keep balance for living.

Inside and Outside is One and the Same.

Your brain has immense capacity.

I wonder why people's are mostly interesting to see the wonders of man made things but forgot about themselves!

Human body's structure is Incredible of Incredibles! Wonder of Wonders!

Nature has constructed the whole molecular structure of everything.

So, everything is complete molecular structure of nature itself.

So you are.

So everything is god.

God is everywhere.

So, you are also god.

Every living being is god.

You are a complete molecular structure of god.

Love is god.

Nature loves you always.

-/-
/-/

Life Depends On Nature

We all know about sangam landscape :-

1. Mountain region : Life depends upon mountain.

2. Forest region : Life depends upon forest.

3. Crop land : Life depends upon crop field.

4. Sea shore : Life depends upon sea.

5. Desert : Life depends upon desert.

Where we are all living ?

What land we are all depending ?

We are all depend upon machines.

We are all depends upon nonliving things.

We are all depends upon thoughts.

That's why chaos spread all over the world.

No on is depend upon living things.

Life is depends on living things only not non
living things.

Life depends on nature, living things not non living things.

When we are all depends upon nature then life is begin.

When we depends on nature that's we are living otherwise we are dead.

Already we pollute air, so many noise pollution it is cause of not peace.

Peace comes when our life depends on nature.

Already we caused our planet global warming is our biggest tragedy.

Most of species died in every minute cause of global warming.

It is time to reconsider of nature, this world.

It is time to reunion with nature.

This universe and all creatures body including humans are one and same.

All lives are depends on this marvellous earth, air, water, sun, moon.

We are not separate from this earth, universe.

We are this world or universe.

This universe and all creatures body including humans are one and the same.

All lives depends on this marvellous earth, universe.

We are not separated from this earth, universe.

We are this world, universe.

If we separate ourselves from nature then life
is misery.

If we unite with nature then life is bliss.

When we all depend upon nature then life begins.

Already we lost our consciousness.

We L ost touch with nature.

Already we pollute air, water and create so
many noice pollution.

We are all depends on the major five elements.
If we pollute all elements then how can we live?
We are not separate from five elements. We are five
elements altogether.

Universe and being is one and the same.

Please think it out and reunite with nature.

Save our nature which means save ourselves.

Remember who we are?

We are universe.

Otherwise all will be lost.

Reconsider humanity.

Not only human being but consider about
every being.

This world is home for all beings not only humans.

Otherwise we lost our family.

This universe is our home.

every being is childrens of universe.

Only humans can understand truth.

Thats why humans body is very rare body,

only we can understand what is truth.

Aware of who you are.

Aware of who we are.

Aware of every other being.

We are one and the same.

Every being is one and the same.

Every other beings is our relatives.

We are all child of this universe.

This world is our home.

Every creatures is our kith and kin.

Save our home.

Save our relatives.

It is time to reunion with consciousness.

B ecause we are all one and the same.

(Being - Consciousness - Bliss)

-/-
/-/

<u>Realize Who You Are!</u>
<u>FIND THE SOURCE</u>

Everything in this world is nothing but just a
reflection of the source.

There is no reflection without the source, no matter whatever it is.

Whether it is gold nor diamond or you nor I and so on.. The reflections are many but the source is only one. The reflection of the source is one though many.

If the darkness thrives the world, in this absence of light, nothing is called, even pearl or diamond or gold or platinum no matter what it is!.

Its simply does not matter.

Only in the presence of light, we value everything which is nothing, simply nonsense.

Whether it is gold or diamond.

It glitters but how?

What makes it to shine?

But it could not shine.

Gold or diamond whatever it is do not shine idiot, they refract.

They only refract the light.

All that matters is only the reflection of the light, that is the source.

All that glitters is not gold.

Which means : gold is purity, purity of light.

Light is only pure.

All others are nothing but a glitter of the light/ only reflection/ refraction.

All that glitters is not gold.

Which means : All that reflection is not the source.

We are so engrossed with the objects, or appearances revealed by the light, that we pay no attention to the light.

How can we value which is something valueless.

Even money also.

It is made of paper.

Just paper and is easily futile.

How could we value paper, more than the tree?

What is the source of paper?

How it is made?

Tree! Is not it?

But we destroy tree for what?

For money! Is not it?

We destroy tree and make paper and value it by money. We destroy living things and create non living things.

We value the non living things, more than the living things.

How ridiculous is the way of living?

If we value something, then we should value everything equally.

If we value gold, then we must equally value pebble.

What is gold?

It is just one of the minerals of sand.

It is just sand.

What is diamond?

It is also one of the minerals of stone.

It is just stone.

How could we value sand or is stone more
valuable than man?

How ridicule? How stupid? We are!.

How could we value non living things more
than living things.

What kind of living is this?

If anyone humans are intelligence, then every humans
are also intelligence in their own way.

If anyone humans are idiot, then every humans are
also idiot in their own way.

There is no comparison.

We are all have one sun, one moon, one earth.

We are all living this universe.

If you have any power or intelligence something than
every being is equally have.

Because we are all have the same source.

Then, How could man rules another man, man slaves
another man?

How could man praise or blame another man?

If we praise any man, then every man is equally praised.

But see what we are doing? How ridicule? What kind of stupid living we live?

So much of stupidity.

If we value anything, then everything should be equally valued. If we don't value anything, then everything should be valueless. Because all are just made of the source.

Just reflection/ refraction of the source.

How could we value something only by reflection?

We only consider the reflection but not always are considering the source.

What kind of life, we are living? Stupidity!.

Find the source.

If you find the source, you will know that all the reflections are within the source.

When you realize this, all the reflections will suddenly vanish.

Then only the source will remain still forever!.

-/

Awaken Mind

Mind is totally awaken.

complete attention, Seeing, listening, observing.

Just witnessing, watching, alertness, mindfulness.

present state is only exist otherwise all are imagination.

In that present state mind is completely still, calm, quietness, fearless, bliss, peace.

In the present state is never old.

In the present state is always a new, a fresh and young.

In the present state is not a continuity of the past.

In the present state is timeless.

In the present state is stateless.

In the present moment is not movement of anything.

In the present moment is inevitable changes.

In the present moment is living and dying happening simultaneously.

In the present moment is complete attention, seeing, listening.

In the present moment is not seeking.

In the present moment is not demanding.

In the present moment is not asking.

In the present moment is not judging.

In the present moment is not prejudice.

In the present moment is never thought.

In the present moment is not identification of anything.

In the present moment is neither body nor mind.

In the present moment is neither you nor i.

In the present moment is not thinking.

In the present moment is not fantasy.

In the present moment is fearless.

In the present moment is painless.

In the present moment is no sorrow.

In the present moment is joy.

In the present moment is never born and never die.

In the present moment is completely still.

In the present moment is not a moment.

In the present is not a present but only presence.

It is eternal.

Now I am clear about all our lives are nothing but thought.

Now we clear about we are all living in thought.

All stories they telling like identifying yourself this and that, the world, the society, including families everything you taught by others, everything you known is nothing but thought. Except real thing. Real thing is living, alive.

Yesterday, today, tomorrow are all nothing but thought.

Past, present, future is nothing but thoughts. Thought is time.

All dramas are made by human thoughts.

Every human being is sleeping and dreaming continuously because they just followed millions of era growing by stories like tradition, religion, country and so on. They just doing the same thing to you and your children after children going on telling the fancy stories of thought keep you asleep and make dreams more.

No one can awake you until yourself that is a big tragedy.

Only self enquiry helps you awaken.

Self enquiry is the one, infallible means, the only direct one, to realize the unconditioned, absolute being that you really are!

Desire is the root cause of all. Because desire is also thought.

Thought play all the games. Thought plays huge game in our life. Thought is memory, thought is image, thought is thinking, thought is knowledge, thought is experience, thought is pain, thought is sorrow, thought is pleasure, thought is fear.

All our life is huge filled with thoughts. Thought is fully occupied our life. We don't have space.

Only Truth can liberate you.

And that Truth can be discovered by yourself.

Only self enquiry can rid of all thoughts.

Let go of all thought.

Enter into the thoughtless state.

All forms are disappeared and enter into the formless.

Enter into the void.

Enter into the vast space of silence.

Let silence take you to the core of life.

-/-
/-/

<u>TAO</u> :-

To the mind that is still, the whole universe
surrenders.

when there is silence one finds the anchor of the
universe within oneself.

Why do you run around looking for the truth?

Be still, and there it is

in the mountain,

In the sea,

In the tree,

in the sky,

In yourself.

<u>BUDDHA</u> :-

Silence is an empty space. Space is the home of the
awakened mind.

Nothing ever exists entirely alone; everything is in relation to everything else.

The way is not in the book, not in the sky; the way is in the heart.

There is no salvation without compassion of every other beings.

Peace comes from within. Do not seek it without.

We can never obtain peace in the outer world until we make peace with ourselves.

No one saves us but ourselves. No one can and no one may. We ourselves must walk the path.

RUMI :-

This silence, this moment, every moment, if it's genuinely inside you, brings what you need. There is nothing to believe. Only when I stopped believing in myself did i come in to this beauty.

Live in silence.

When i am silent, I fall in to the place where everything is music.

Why are you so afraid of silence. Silence is the root of everything.

Keep silent, because the world of silence is a vast fullness.

CONFUCIUS :-

Everything has beauty, but not everyone sees it.

"Learn how to see. Realise that everything is connects to everything else."

<u>**Ramana Maharishi**</u> :-

The only language, that is able to express the whole truth is Silence.

The state free from thoughts is the only real state.

All that is required to realize the self is to be still.

Silence is Truth.

Silence is Bliss.

Silence is Peace.

Hence Silence is the Self.

Be quiet that is Truth; Be still that is God.

All are seeing god always. But they do not know it.

Your own Self realization is the greatest service you can render the world.

Transforming yourself is a means of giving light to the whole world.

The only useful purpose of the present birth is to turn within and realize the self. There is nothing else to do.

When you transcend the body - consciousness, the "others" also disappear. The realized one doesn't see the world as different from himself.

Diversity lies in your imagination only. Unitary being need not be acquired.

NANAK :-

What should you have to fear. Trees, plants and all that is inside and outside is he himself.

VIVEKANANDA :-

Where can we go to find god if we cannot see him in our hearts and in every living being.

Immanuel Kant :-

Science is organised knowledge.

Wisdom is organised life.

EINSTEIN :-

Nature is not a by product of god. Nature is god. Science without religion is lame. Religion without science is blind.

NIKOLA TESLA :-

What one man calls god and another calls the law of physics.

Jiddu Krishnamurti :-

It is beautiful to be alone. To be alone doesn't mean to be lonely. It means the mind is not influenced and contaminated by the society.

It is good to be alone. To be far away from the world and yet walk its streets is to be alone. To be alone walking up the path beside the rushing, noisy mountain stream full of spring water and melting snows is to be aware of that solitary tree, alone in its beauty.

A human being, if he transforms himself, become alone, but that aloneness is not isolation - it is a form of supreme intelligence.

Awareness is silent observation without choice, condemnation or justification.

Awareness is the silent and choiceless observation of 'what is'.when one is deeply conscious or aware, there is remnant or hidden unconscious movement. There is no division between the inner and the outer.

<u>OSHO</u> :-

Remember, aloneness is not loneliness.

Have you ever thought about this beautiful word, alone?

It means all one.

It is made of two words all and one.

In aloneness you become one with the all.

Awareness means to be in the moment, so that totally there is no movement towards the past, no movement towards the future - all movements stops.

There is no other greater ecstasy, than to know who you are.

Find ecstasy within yourself. It is not out there.
It is in your innermost flowering. The you are
looking for is you.